Clown

Luk Depondt – Guido Van Genechten

meadowside
CHILDREN'S BOOKS

he wildest horses,

and stroke the fiercest of lions.

and march through
the roaring rains.

I'd walk on the tightest of tightropes,

then march
out to make
them all
laugh!

Meadowside Children's Books
185 Fleet Street London EC4A 2HS

This edition published 2006
Text © Luk Depondt 2000
Illustrations © Guido Van Genechten 2000
The rights of Luk Depondt to be identified
as the author and Guido Van Genechten
as the illustrator of this work have been
asserted by them in accordance with the
Copyright, Designs and Patents Act, 1988

A CIP catalogue record for this book is available
is available from the British Library
10 9 8 7 6 5 4 3 2 1
Printed in China

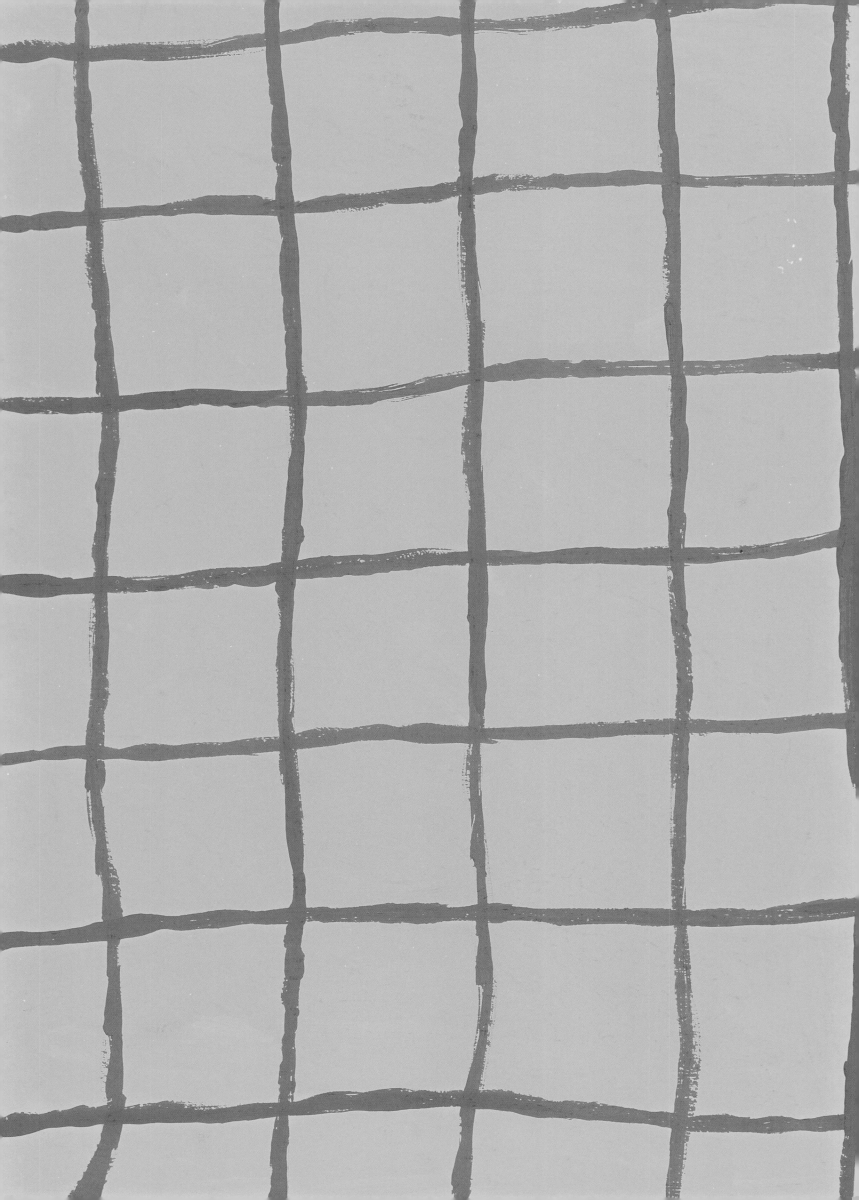